TIMELESS CLASSICS

DR. JEKYLL AND MR. HYDE

Robert Louis Stevenson

– ADAPTED BY –

Janice Greene

SADDLEBACK
EDUCATIONAL PUBLISHING

TIMELESS CLASSICS

Literature Set 1 (1719-1844)

A Christmas Carol
The Count of Monte Cristo
Frankenstein
Gulliver's Travels
The Hunchback of Notre Dame
The Last of the Mohicans

Oliver Twist
Pride and Prejudice
Robinson Crusoe
The Swiss Family Robinson
The Three Musketeers

Literature Set 2 (1845-1884)

The Adventures of Huckleberry Finn
The Adventures of Tom Sawyer
Around the World in 80 Days
Great Expectations
Jane Eyre
The Man in the Iron Mask

Moby Dick
The Prince and the Pauper
The Scarlet Letter
A Tale of Two Cities
20,000 Leagues Under the Sea

Literature Set 3 (1886-1908)

The Call of the Wild
Captains Courageous
Dracula
Dr. Jekyll and Mr. Hyde
The Hound of the Baskervilles
The Jungle Book

Kidnapped
The Red Badge of Courage
The Time Machine
Treasure Island
The War of the Worlds
White Fang

SADDLEBACK
EDUCATIONAL PUBLISHING
www.sdlback.com

ISBN: 978-1-61651-076-3
eBook: 978-1-60291-810-8

Printed in the United States

25 24 23 22 21   6 7 8 9 10

TIMELESS CLASSICS

Contents

| 1 |

A Very Odd Story

Mr. Utterson the lawyer was a rugged-looking man. His face rarely lit up in a smile. His conversation was cold, brief, and embarrassed. People saw him as lean, long, dusty, and dreary. Yet he could sometimes be lovable. At friendly meetings—and when the wine was to his taste—something wonderfully human shone from his eye. At these times one could see an inviting warmth in his face.

He was quite strict with himself. Though he enjoyed the theater, he had not attended a play for 20 years. But he was easygoing with others. He used to say, "I let my brother go to the devil in his own way."

Mr. Utterson was rather shy. He did not seek out friends, but welcomed those who came his way. His friends were those of his own blood, or those whom he had known the longest.

This, no doubt, was the bond that united him to Mr. Richard Enfield. He was a distant cousin, and a well-known man about town. Their friendship was a nut to crack for many. What could these two see in each other? What subject could they find in common? People said that when they met Mr. Utterson and Mr. Enfield on their Sunday walks, the two men said nothing. Yet for all that, both men counted their walks as the chief jewel of the week.

By chance, one of these walks led them down a back street in a busy part of London. The street was small, but on the weekdays it was very busy. The shop fronts had an inviting air, as if they were rows of smiling saleswomen. Even on Sunday, when it was almost empty, the street shone out in contrast to its dingy neighborhood.

But on the east side, there was a certain sinister building. It was two stories high. There were no windows, only a door with no bell or knocker. Tramps slouched against it and struck matches on the panels. A schoolboy had tried his knife on the molding. For close to a generation, no one had bothered to drive away these destructive visitors, or to repair their damage.

As the men walked by the door, Mr. Enfield pointed to it with his cane. "Did you ever notice that door before?" he asked. "It is connected in my mind with a very odd story."

Mr. Utterson's voice changed slightly. He said, "Indeed? And what was that?"

"I was on my way home from a long journey," Mr. Enfield said. "It was about three o'clock on a black winter morning. The streets were so empty that I began to long for the sight of a policeman. All at once I saw two figures: One was a little man walking along quickly. The other was a girl of eight or ten. She was running as fast as she could down a cross street.

"Well, naturally, the man and the girl ran into each other at the corner. But then came the horrible part of the thing. The man trampled right over the child's body! He left her screaming on the ground. It may sound like nothing to hear, but I assure you it was a hellish thing to see!

"I took to my heels and seized the man by the collar. When I brought him back to where he'd left the child, there was already quite a group around her.

"The people who had turned out were the child's own family. They had sent for a doctor who had just arrived. Well, the child was not much the worse for the fall. She was more frightened than anything else. And there you might have supposed this strange event would have ended.

"But there was one curious point. I had taken a loathing to the hateful man at first sight. So had the child's family—which was only natural. But the doctor's behavior was what struck me. He was the usual cut and dried doctor. He had a strong Edinburgh accent, and was about as emotional as a bagpipe.

"Well, sir, when he turned to my prisoner, he went white and looked as if he wanted to kill him! I knew what was in his mind, just as he knew what was in mine. Since killing him was ridiculous, we decided to do the next best thing.

"We told the man we would make a scandal out of this. We promised that we would make his name stink from one end of London to the other.

If he had any friends or any credit, we would make sure that he lost them. At the same time, we were keeping the women off him as best we could. They were as wild as harpies.

"I never saw such a circle of angry faces. And there was the little man in the middle. He had a kind of black, sneering coldness. He was frightened, I could see that—but carrying it off boldly, like Satan."

" 'No gentleman wants to make a scene,' said the man. 'Name your figure.' Well, we

9

screwed him up to a hundred pounds for the child's family. And where do you think he took us but to that place with the door? He whipped out a key and went in. Soon he came out with ten pounds in gold and a check for the rest. The check was signed with a name I can't mention—but it's a name that's very well known.

"I told the man that the whole business seemed suspicious. In real life, a man does not walk into a cellar door at four in the morning—and come out of it with another man's check for close to a hundred pounds!

"But the man was quite easy about it. He sneered, 'Set your mind at rest. I will stay with you until the banks open and cash the check myself.' So we all set off, the doctor, the child's father, the strange man, and myself. We passed the night in my chambers. The next day after breakfast, the four of us went to the bank. Obviously, I had every reason to believe that the check would be a forgery. But not a bit of it. The check was genuine."

Mr. Utterson said, "Tut-tut."

"Yes, it's a bad story," Mr. Enfield went on. "For the man was really a *damnable* fellow! But the one who wrote the check is a very good and honest man. I suppose it must be blackmail. An honest man must be paying through the nose for something he did in his youth."

Mr. Utterson said, "Do you know if the person who wrote the check lives beyond that door?"

"It seems a likely place, doesn't it?" Mr. Enfield replied. "But no, I happened to notice his address. He lives in some square or another."

"There's one point I want to clear up," said Utterson. "May I ask the name of the man who walked over the child?"

"Well," said Mr. Enfield, "I can't see what harm it would do after all this time. It was a man by the name of Hyde."

"Hmmm," said Mr. Utterson. "What sort of a man is he to see?"

"He is not an easy man to describe," said Enfield. "There is something wrong with his appearance—something that is downright *detestable*. I never saw a man I disliked more, yet I hardly know why. He gives a strong feeling of deformity. Yet there is no exact deformity I can name. But I could never forget his face. In my mind's eye, I can see him at this moment!"

"You'll find this strange," Mr. Utterson said. "But I won't ask you the name of the man who wrote the check. You see, my dear fellow—I already know it."

"Huh!" Mr. Enfield's voice now took on an edge of annoyance. "Well, you might have warned me!" he sputtered. "Perhaps I would have been wiser to say nothing. Let us make a bargain never to refer to this matter again!"

Mr. Utterson said, "I agree with all my heart. Let us shake hands on that, Richard."

| 2 |

Mr. Seek Meets Mr. Hyde

That evening, Mr. Utterson came home in a dark mood. He sat down to dinner but had no appetite. Usually on Sunday, he read by the fire until midnight and then went to bed. On this night, however, he took up a candle and went to his study. There he opened his safe and took out a document. The title read *Last Will and Testament*.

He studied the will with a frown. It stated that in case of Dr. Henry Jekyll's death, all of his money and property would go to his friend, Edward Hyde. And if Dr. Jekyll ever disappeared for more than three months, Edward Hyde should take over his affairs without delay.

To make out such a will seemed madness. After Enfield's story about Edward Hyde, Utterson feared for his friend Jekyll.

Mr. Utterson was worried. He put the will back in his safe, blew out the candle, and went out to see his friend Dr. Lanyon.

Dr. Lanyon sat alone in his dining room, drinking a glass of wine. He was a healthy, red-faced, white-haired gentleman, with a decided manner. At the sight of Mr. Utterson, Dr. Lanyon sprang from his chair and welcomed him.

After a little rambling talk, Utterson said, "I suppose, Lanyon, that you and I must be the two oldest friends Henry Jekyll has?"

Dr. Lanyon chuckled. "I wish the friends were younger," he said, "but I suppose we are. And what of that? Actually, I see little of Jekyll now."

"Really?" asked Mr. Utterson.

"More than ten years ago, Dr. Jekyll became too strange for me," Lanyon went on. "He began to go *wrong* somehow—wrong in his mind, you see. Such scientific balderdash he got into! Anyway, I've seen devilish little of the man."

Mr. Utterson felt relieved. He told himself that they must have argued only on some point of science. It was nothing worse than that!

"Did you ever meet a friend of his—a Mr. Hyde?" he asked curiously.

"Hyde? No. Never heard of him," Dr. Lanyon said.

As Mr. Utterson walked back to his home, his mind was full of questions. All night he tossed on his bed. When the clock struck six, Utterson's mind was filled with images of Hyde. As he lay in the darkness, Enfield's story went before his eyes in a scroll of pictures. He could imagine the lights of the city at night. Then he could see a child running into the man, and the man walking over her—in spite of her screams.

Next, Mr. Utterson would see a room in a rich house, where Dr. Jekyll lay asleep. Jekyll was dreaming, and smiling at his dreams. Then the curtains of his bed were drawn apart, and Hyde peered in. So even at that dead hour, Jekyll had to rise from his bed and do Hyde's bidding.

As he dozed, Utterson saw Hyde glide silently though sleeping houses. He seemed to move swiftly, and then even more swiftly. At every corner he crushed a child and left her screaming.

But the man Utterson imagined had no face. He felt if he could only *see* the face of the real Mr. Hyde, perhaps the mystery would fade away completely.

From that day on, Mr. Utterson haunted the door in the little back street. Always he said to himself, "If he be Mr. Hyde, I shall be Mr. Seek."

Then at last his patience was rewarded. It was a fine, dry night. Frost was in the air. Mr. Utterson had been standing some minutes at his spot, when he heard an odd, light footstep drawing near. Moving quickly, Utterson stepped out of sight in a doorway and watched the street.

He saw a small man, very plainly dressed. The man walked quickly up to the door and took a key from his pocket.

Mr. Utterson stepped out of the shadows and touched the man's shoulder. He said, "Mr. Hyde, I think?"

Mr. Hyde shrank back, sucking in his breath with a hiss. But he answered coolly enough, "That is my name, sir. What is it that you want?"

"I am an old friend of Dr. Jekyll's. My name is Utterson. Since I've run into you, I thought you might ask me in."

Turning away, Mr. Hyde unlocked the door. He said, "You will not find Dr. Jekyll in," he said. "I'm afraid he has gone out."

"Will you do me a small favor, sir?" Mr. Utterson asked.

"With pleasure," said Mr. Hyde politely. "What shall it be?"

"Will you let me see your face?" Mr. Utterson asked. At that Hyde seemed to hesitate. Then he turned around with a defiant look on his face. The two men stared at each other.

"Now I shall know you if we meet again," Mr. Utterson said with a smile.

"Yes," said Mr. Hyde. "It is a good thing we have met. And you should have my address as well." He wrote down the number of a street in Soho. Then he asked, "And now, sir—how do you happen to know me?"

Mr. Utterson said, "Oh, yes! Dr. Jekyll told me what you looked like."

"You're *lying*!" cried Mr. Hyde. "Jekyll never told you!"

"Come, come!" said Mr. Utterson. "That is not fitting language, sir."

Mr. Hyde laughed savagely. He turned away.

The next moment, with amazing quickness, he pushed open the door and disappeared into the dark house.

Mr. Utterson put his hand to his brow. He tried to sort out what he had seen. Mr. Hyde was a small, pale man, with an ugly smile. His manner was rather a murderous mixture of boldness and shyness. His voice was hoarse and whispery. But that did not explain the extreme disgust and fear that Utterson felt for him.

"God bless me," Utterson said to himself, "but the man seems hardly human! Oh, my poor Henry! If I ever read Satan's signature upon a face, it is on that of your new friend."

Mr. Utterson walked around the corner to a row of handsome houses. He stopped and knocked at a door that had an air of great wealth and comfort. A well-dressed, elderly butler opened the front door at once.

"Is Dr. Jekyll at home, Poole?" Mr. Utterson asked.

Taking Mr. Utterson's hat, Poole said, "I will see, sir. Will you wait by the fire?"

"Thank you, Poole," said Mr. Utterson.

He stood before the bright fire. The room had always been a favorite of Mr. Utterson's. It had rich oak cabinets and a large, bright open fireplace. But tonight there was a shudder in Utterson's blood. He seemed to read a menace in the flickering shadows of the firelight. He was relieved when Poole returned to say that his master must have gone out.

"Poole," Mr. Utterson said, "I just now saw Mr. Edward Hyde enter the old door to the laboratory. Was that all right—when Doctor Jekyll is out?"

"It's quite all right with my master," said Poole. "Mr. Hyde has a key."

"Your master seems to have a great deal of trust in Mr. Hyde."

"Yes, he does," said Poole. "We've all had orders to obey him."

After saying goodnight to Poole, Mr. Utterson walked home with a heavy heart. "Poor Henry Jekyll," he said to himself. "He said he was wild when he was young. This must be the ghost of some old sin, come back to haunt him."

But then he saw a spark of hope. "This Mr. Hyde must have secrets of his own," he thought.

"Secrets that make poor Jekyll's worst sins look like sunshine. But no matter. Things cannot go on like this. If Hyde learns of the will, he may try to bring on Jekyll's death. I will do all I can to stop this creature—if Jekyll will only let me." Then, remembering the strange will that Jekyll had insisted on writing, Mr. Utterson let out a deep sigh.

| 3 |

Another Vicious Attack

By excellent good fortune, Dr. Jekyll soon gave one of his pleasant dinners for five or six old friends. Utterson stayed behind after the other guests had gone. Jekyll had often asked him to stay. After the lighthearted and loose-tongued guests had gone, he liked the silent companionship of the old lawyer.

Dr. Jekyll now sat opposite Mr. Utterson before the fire. The doctor was a large, well-built man of 50. He was a stylish man, and had every mark of kindness on his face.

Mr. Utterson began, "I have been wanting to speak to you, Jekyll. You know that will of yours?"

"My poor Utterson!" laughed Jekyll. "I never saw a man so unhappy as you are about my will."

"I've learned something alarming about your Mr. Hyde," Mr. Utterson said.

The large, handsome face of Dr. Jekyll grew pale, even to the lips. He said, "I do not care to hear more. This is a matter I thought we had agreed to drop."

"What I heard about him was terrible," said Mr. Utterson.

"I will make no change in the will," the doctor said. "You do not understand my position. It is one of those affairs that cannot be mended by talking."

"Jekyll," said Mr. Utterson, "you know me—I am a man to be trusted. Tell me what has happened. No doubt I can get you out of whatever trouble you are in."

"My good Utterson," said the doctor, "I cannot find words to thank you. But this isn't what you imagine. It's not as bad as that. Just to put your good heart at rest, I will tell you one thing—at any moment I choose, I can be rid of Hyde. I give you my hand on that. Now, I beg of you to let the matter sleep."

Utterson looked unhappily into the fire. At last he said, "Very well, Jekyll." Then he stood up as if to leave.

"There is one last point I should like you to understand," Dr. Jekyll went on. "I do sincerely take a great—a *very* great—interest in young Mr. Hyde. If I am taken away, Utterson, promise me that you will help him. Please make sure he gets all I have left to him. I know you would—if you knew everything. It would be a weight off my mind if you would promise."

"I can't pretend that I shall ever *like* the man," said Mr. Utterson with a frown.

"I don't ask that," said Dr. Jekyll. "I only ask

for fairness. I only ask you to help him—for my sake—when I am no longer here."

Utterson could not help but sigh. "I promise," he said.

* * * *

A year after Utterson had made his promise, London was shocked by a terrible crime. The details were few and strange. At 11:00 P.M., a young maid had gone upstairs to her bedroom. But before going to bed she had stopped to look out at the moon. It was full and brilliant that night.

At the window the maid noticed a white-haired gentleman walking down the lane. Quickly coming up the opposite way was a small man. When the two men came near one another, the older one bowed and spoke to the younger man. He appeared to be asking directions. The young maid smiled as she watched, for the white-haired gentleman seemed to have gentle, old-world manners.

Then, in the bright moonlight, she noticed that the small man was Mr. Hyde. He had once visited her master, and she had disliked him. This night Mr. Hyde held a heavy cane in his hand. He seemed to listen to the older man with impatience.

All at once Mr. Hyde broke out in a great burst of anger. He waved his cane like a madman. Shocked, the old gentleman stepped back. At that, Mr. Hyde clubbed him to the earth. Then, with apelike fury, he trampled the old man under his feet and beat him savagely with his cane. The maid heard the old man's bones shatter under the heavy blows. At the horror of these sights and sounds, the poor girl fainted.

It was 2:00 A.M. before the maid came to herself and called the police. The murderer was long gone. But his mangled victim still lay in the street. The cane had broken in two. Half of it lay in the gutter. The other half, without doubt, had been carried away by the murderer.

A purse and a fine gold watch were found on the victim—along with a letter addressed to Mr. Utterson.

The letter was brought to the old lawyer the next morning. When he saw it, he said, "I shall say nothing more until I have seen the body."

Utterson hurried through breakfast. Then he drove to the police station, where the body had been carried. As soon as he saw the murdered man he said, "I recognize him! I am sorry to say that this is Sir Danvers Carew, the M.P."

The police officer exclaimed, "Good God, sir. Is it possible? Perhaps you can help us find the murderer." The officer told Utterson the maid's story. When he mentioned Hyde's name, Utterson's heart sank. Then the officer showed Utterson the broken cane.

Utterson recognized the cane. Many years ago he had given it to Henry Jekyll. Now he turned to the police officer and said, "Please come with me in my cab. I think I can take you to Mr. Hyde's house."

They drove to Soho, and turned down a dingy street where ragged children huddled in doorways. This was the home of Henry Jekyll's favorite—the man who was heir to his fortune.

A silver-haired old woman opened the door. Utterson saw right away that her face was evil—made smoother by hypocrisy. But her manners were excellent. Yes, she said, this was indeed the home of Mr. Hyde. But he was not in at the moment.

"Very well, then," said Utterson. "We wish to see his rooms. This is Inspector Newcomen of Scotland Yard."

A flash of ugly joy brightened the woman's face. "Ah!" she said. "Is he in trouble, then? What has he done?"

Mr. Utterson and the inspector exchanged glances. "He don't seem a very popular character," the inspector whispered. "Come on, Utterson. Let's have a look about."

The rooms were furnished in luxury and good taste. A closet was filled with wine; the carpets were thick and agreeable in color; a handsome picture hung on the wall. But the rooms also looked as though they had recently been ransacked. Clothes lay about on the floor. Drawers stood open. On the hearth lay a pile of gray ashes. Looking through the ashes, the inspector found a portion of a green checkbook. Then Utterson found the other half of the broken cane behind the door.

The inspector said, "You may depend on it, sir. I have this man Hyde in my hand. Why, money is *life* to the man. We have only to wait for him at the bank."

This was not so simple, however. There was no trace of Hyde's family. Few people knew him. Those who had seen him had different ideas of what he looked like. They agreed on only one point: There was something about Mr. Hyde that seemed *terribly wrong*.

| 4 |
A New Life for Jekyll

It was late in the afternoon by the time Utterson found his way to Dr. Jekyll's door. When Poole let him in, Utterson hurried to the doctor's laboratory. There Dr. Jekyll sat by a fire, looking deadly sick. He did not rise to greet his friend, but held out a cold hand to welcome him. Even his voice seemed sick.

As soon as Poole left them alone, Mr. Utterson asked, "Have you heard the news?"

The doctor shuddered. "Yes," he said. "The newsboys were calling about it in the square. I heard them from my dining room."

"Carew was my client," said Utterson, "—but so are you. I want to know what you are doing. You have not been fool enough to hide this mad fellow, have you?"

"Utterson, I swear to God," said Dr. Jekyll. "*I swear to God* I will never set eyes on him again! I bid my honor that I am done with him. And indeed, Hyde does not *want* my help. You do not know him as I do. Mark my words, you will never hear of him again."

Mr. Utterson listened gloomily. He did not like his friend's feverish manner. "You seem pretty sure of him," he said. "For *your* sake, I hope you are right. If this murder came to trial, your name might appear."

"I am quite sure of him," said Dr. Jekyll. "But I must ask your advice. I have—I have received a letter today. I am at a loss whether I should show it to the police. I should like to leave it in *your* hands, Utterson."

Utterson examined the letter, which was written in an odd, upright hand. It was signed *Edward Hyde*. In it, Hyde thanked Jekyll for all the help he had given him. He urged the doctor not to worry about his safety, for he had a sure means of escape.

Mr. Utterson liked this letter well enough. It showed that Dr. Jekyll and Mr. Hyde were not as close as he had feared. "Shall I keep this letter?" he asked.

"Please," said the doctor. "Decide for yourself what to do with it. Just now I have no confidence in myself."

"Well, I shall consider it," said Mr. Utterson. "And now, one word more. It was Hyde, was it not, who made you write those terms in your will—that he would inherit your fortune if you disappeared?"

Dr. Jekyll looked as if he might faint. He took a deep breath and nodded.

"I knew it," said Utterson. "He meant to murder you. You've had a lucky escape."

"I have had much more than that," Dr. Jekyll said. "I have had a *lesson*. Oh, God, Utterson—what a lesson I have had!"

On his way out, Utterson spoke to the butler. "By the way, Poole—Dr. Jekyll received a letter today. Do you remember what the messenger looked like?"

But Poole was absolutely sure that no letter was delivered that day.

With this surprising news, Utterson began to worry once more. He found himself longing for someone to give him advice.

Soon after, Utterson was back home with his head clerk, Mr. Guest. There was no man Utterson kept fewer secrets from than Mr. Guest. Having often been on business at Dr. Jekyll's, Guest knew Poole well. Also, he was a great student and critic of handwriting.

Utterson showed him the letter, which Guest studied with passionate interest. At last he said, "It is an odd hand."

"—and by all accounts a very odd writer," added Utterson.

Just then a servant entered with a note for Mr. Utterson.

"Is that from Dr. Jekyll, sir?" Mr. Guest asked. "I thought I knew the writing. Anything private, Mr. Utterson?"

"No, it's only an invitation to dinner," Mr. Utterson said. "Why? Do you want to see it?"

The clerk laid the letter and the invitation side by side to compare them. "There's a strong resemblance," he said. "The two hands are in many ways identical, only differently sloped."

"If I were you, I wouldn't speak of this note to anyone," Utterson said.

"No, sir," said Guest. "I understand."

No sooner was Mr. Utterson alone that night than he locked the note in his safe. "My God!" he said to himself. "Henry Jekyll forged a letter for a murderer!" He staggered to his chair. His blood was running cold in his veins.

* * * *

Time went by. Thousands of pounds were offered in reward for the murderer of Sir Danvers Carew. But it was as if Mr. Hyde had never existed. Much of his past was found out. Tales were told of the man's evil ways and his cold and violent cruelty. But there was not a whisper of where he might be now. From the time he had left the house in Soho on the morning of the murder, he was simply blotted out.

As time went on, Mr. Utterson became less worried and was more at ease with himself. To his way of thinking, the death of Sir Danvers Carew was more than paid for by the disappearance of Mr. Hyde.

And now that Hyde was gone, a new life had begun for Dr. Jekyll. He spent time with his friends. Once more he was a familiar guest and host. He was busy at his work and he did good deeds. Somehow his face seemed to open and brighten. For more than two months, the doctor was at peace.

On the 8th of January, Mr. Utterson dined at Dr. Jekyll's house. Lanyon was there, too. It was just like the old days when the three men were the closest of friends.

But on the 12th of January, Dr. Jekyll shut his door to Mr. Utterson. Poole told him, "The doctor is seeing no one." Mr. Utterson tried again and again. He had grown used to seeing his old friend every day. Jekyll's return to solitude began to weigh heavily on Utterson's spirits. Finally, he went to visit Dr. Lanyon.

Utterson was shocked at the change in the doctor's looks. A death warrant was plainly written on his friend's face. The rosy man had grown pale. His flesh had fallen away. He was balder and much older looking. But more than this, the look in his eye spoke of some deep terror in his mind.

"I have had a shock," Dr. Lanyon told Utterson, "and I fear I shall never recover. It is only a question of weeks before I go. Well, Utterson, my life has been pleasant—I liked it—yes, sir, I *used to* like it."

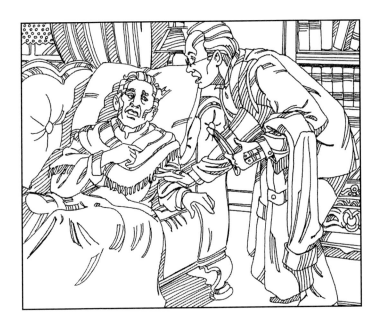

"I'm sorry, Lanyon. Dr. Jekyll is ill, too. Have you seen him?" Mr. Utterson asked in a worried voice.

Lanyon's face changed, and he held up a trembling hand. He said, "I wish to see or hear no more of Jekyll! I am quite done with that person. I beg you not to speak of him."

"Tut-tut," said Mr. Utterson. "Can't anything be done? After all, we three are very old friends, Lanyon. We shall not live to make others."

"Nothing can be done," said Lanyon coldly. "Ask him yourself."

"He will not see me," said Mr. Utterson.

"I'm not surprised at that," Dr. Lanyon said. "Someday, after I am dead, you may learn the right and wrong of this. There is nothing more that I can tell you."

| 5 |

A Prisoner in His Own Home

After his visit with Lanyon, Mr. Utterson wrote to Dr. Jekyll. He complained about not being allowed to visit. He also asked the reason for breaking off his friendship with Lanyon. The next day he received a reply.

Dr. Jekyll wrote that the break with Lanyon could not be mended. He said, "I do not blame our old friend. But I share his view that we must never meet again. My life from now on must be very secluded. Do not be surprised if my door is often shut—even to you. But never doubt our friendship.

"You must let me go my own dark way. I have brought on a punishment and a danger

I cannot name. If I am the chief of sinners, I am also the chief of sufferers. There is only one way you can help me, Utterson. And that is to respect my silence."

Utterson was amazed. A week ago he had seen Dr. Jekyll cheerful and smiling. Now it seemed that the man's life was doomed.

A week later, Dr. Lanyon took to his bed. Less than two weeks after that, he was dead. The night after the funeral, Utterson locked the door of his study. He got out an envelope that was addressed by Dr. Lanyon. It said, *PRIVATE: To be read by G.J. Utterson ALONE*. Mr. Utterson broke the seal of the envelope. Inside was another envelope. It said, "Not to be opened until the death or disappearance of Dr. Henry Jekyll."

Utterson was very curious. He longed to break the seal and dive at once to the bottom of these mysteries. But his own honor and loyalty to his dead friend held him back.

Although he locked up Lanyon's letter unread, Utterson's curiosity was still strong. Several times he went to call on Dr. Henry Jekyll. Every time he was turned away. Perhaps it was a relief after all that he could not see

Henry Jekyll. The doctor had grown so strange and difficult to understand! Perhaps in his heart Utterson found it easier to stand in the open air, talking to Poole, than to enter the home where Jekyll kept himself a prisoner.

Poole had no good news to tell Utterson. It appeared that Dr. Jekyll spent most of his days in the laboratory. Sometimes he even slept there. He had become very silent. He did not read. It seemed he had something on his mind. Utterson became used to hearing the same news from Poole every time he tried to visit. Little by little, he fell off coming to Jekyll's house.

One Sunday, Utterson was out on his usual walk with Mr. Enfield. By chance, their walk led them to the old back door of Jekyll's laboratory. They stopped to look at it.

"Well," said Enfield, "at least that story's over. We'll see no more of Mr. Hyde."

"I hope not," Utterson said. "But I'm still worried about poor Jekyll. Let us step into the court and take a look in his windows. I feel that having friends nearby may do him good—even if they are on the outside."

The court was very cool with the coming

night. The sky overhead was bright with sunset. One of the windows was halfway open. Sitting beside it, with the hopeless face of a prisoner, was Dr. Jekyll.

Mr. Utterson cried, "What? Jekyll! I trust you are feeling better."

"I am very low, Utterson," said Jekyll, "very low. It will not last long, thank God."

"You stay too much indoors," said Mr. Utterson. "You should be out, getting your blood moving, like my cousin Enfield and me. Come now, get your hat and take a quick turn with us!"

"You are very good to ask," said Dr. Jekyll. "I should like to very much. But no, no, no—it is quite impossible. I dare not. But indeed, Utterson, I *am* very glad to see you. I would ask you and Mr. Enfield to come in, but the house is really not fit."

Mr. Utterson answered good-naturedly, "Why then, the best thing we can do is stay down here and speak to you."

"That is just what I was going to suggest," said Dr. Jekyll with a smile. But the words were hardly out of his mouth when the smile disappeared from his face. In an instant he wore

a look of such fear and despair that it shocked Utterson into silence. A moment later, Jekyll pulled the window closed.

Without a word, the two men turned and left the court. After they had walked some distance in silence, Mr. Utterson turned and looked at Mr. Enfield. Both men were pale. Horror was in their eyes.

"God forgive us, *God forgive us!*" said Mr. Utterson.

Mr. Enfield nodded. Once more they walked on in silence.

| 6 |

Poole Begs for Help

Half dozing, Utterson was sitting by his fire one evening when he was surprised to receive a visit from Poole.

"Bless me, Poole, what brings you here?" he asked. Then he took a second look at the old servant's face and asked, "What's wrong, man? Is the doctor ill?"

"Yes, Mr. Utterson, I'm afraid there is something *very* wrong."

"Please, sit down, and here is a glass of wine for you," Utterson said kindly. "Now, take your time, and then tell me plainly what I can do to help."

For a long while Poole said nothing, his glass of wine on his knee. Then he said quietly, "I think there's been foul play."

"*Foul play!*" Utterson cried out. "Tell me, man—what do you mean?"

"I dare not say, sir," said Poole. "But will you come along with me? It would be better if you could see for yourself."

Utterson's answer was to quickly get his hat and coat. A look of great relief washed over Poole's face. He put down his wine glass and moved toward the door.

It was a wild, cold night in March. The pale moon lay on her back, as if the wind had tilted her. Mr. Utterson thought he had never seen the streets so empty. He wished very much that there were people about, for his mind was full of dread.

At last they reached Dr. Jekyll's house. Poole knocked and the door was opened on the chain. A voice said, "Is that you, Poole?"

"It's all right," said Poole. "Open the door."

All of Dr. Jekyll's servants were in the hall. They huddled together like a flock of frightened sheep. Seeing Mr. Utterson, the housemaid began to whimper. The cook cried out, "Bless God! It's Mr. Utterson!" She ran forward as if to take him in her arms.

"What! What!" cried Mr. Utterson. "This is not good at all! Your master would not be pleased!"

"They're all afraid," said Poole.

Poole told the gardener's helper to give him a candle. "Now, sir, I'll take you to the laboratory," he said to Mr. Utterson. "Come as quietly as you can. I want you to hear, but I don't want you to be *heard*. And see here, sir, if he was to ask you to come in—don't go."

At these words, Mr. Utterson's nerves started to tremble and jerk. He followed Poole to the laboratory door.

Poole knocked gently. "It's Mr. Utterson, sir," he said, "asking to see you."

A voice from inside the laboratory said, "Tell him I cannot see anyone."

"All right, sir. Thank you," said Poole.

Poole led Utterson out across the yard. Then he looked him in the eye and said, "Tell me, sir, was that my master's voice?"

Mr. Utterson said, "It does seem changed."

"*Changed?*" Poole said. "Well yes, sir, I think so. Haven't I been 20 years in this man's house? Do you think I could be wrong about his voice? No, sir, someone's taken the master away. It was eight days ago that we last heard the master's voice. He was crying out to God to help him. Now I ask you, Mr. Utterson, who's in there, instead of him?"

The old lawyer bit his finger. "This is very strange, Poole," Utterson agreed. "Suppose Dr. Jekyll has been—well, *murdered*. Why would the killer stay here? That doesn't make sense."

Poole said, "All this last week, whoever or whatever lives in that laboratory has been crying out for some sort of medicine. Every day—even twice or three times in one day, he's written these orders. I've been sent flying to all the drugstores in town. Every time I brought the drugs back, he'd throw out a note telling me to return it. He'd say it wasn't pure. Then I'd have to fly out again with another order. This drug is wanted bitter bad, sir, whatever it's for."

Mr. Utterson said, "Have you any of the orders he's written?"

Poole felt in his pocket and brought out a crumpled note. It said, "Unfortunately, this last sample you gave me is impure. Last year I purchased a large quantity from you. I beg you to search carefully to see if any of that quantity is left. If so, please send it to me at once. The cost is of no importance." Then, with a sudden sputter of the pen, he had written, *"For God's sake, find me some of the old drug."*

"This is surely a strange note," said Mr. Utterson. "You're sure that this is Dr. Jekyll's writing, are you not?"

"I thought it was," said Poole. "But what's worse is that I've *seen* him!"

"Seen him?" said Utterson. "Well?"

"It was this way," said Poole. "I came up suddenly from the garden. He had slipped out to see if his drug had been delivered. When he looked around and saw me, he gave a kind of cry and whipped back inside. Sir, if that was my master, why did he have a mask upon his face? Why did he cry out like a rat, and run from me?"

Upset, Poole passed his hand over his face before he could go on. "Sir, that thing was *not* my master. My master is a tall, fine figure of a man. This thing was more like a dwarf. No, sir, that thing in the mask was never Dr. Jekyll. It is the belief of my heart that murder has been done!"

"Then it is my duty to make certain, Poole," Mr. Utterson said. "I think I must break down that door."

"Ah, Mr. Utterson, that's talking!" Poole cried happily. "I can get the axe. And you might take the kitchen poker for yourself."

"Do you realize, Poole, that you and I are about to put ourselves in some danger?" Mr. Utterson asked.

"You may say so, sir, indeed," said Poole.

"Well, then, we must be frank," Mr. Utterson said. "That masked figure you saw—did you recognize it?"

"Well, sir," said Poole, "the thing I saw was very quick, and rather doubled up. But it looked like Mr. Hyde. Have you ever met this Mr. Hyde, sir?"

"Yes," said Mr. Utterson. "I once spoke with him."

Poole said, "Then you know as well as the rest of us that there is *something* about the man that gives you a turn. The sight of that masked thing jumping into the laboratory froze my spine like ice. Oh, I know it's not evidence, Mr. Utterson. But a man has his feelings. I give you my bible-word that it was Mr. Hyde!"

"I believe you," said Mr. Utterson. "I believe poor Henry is killed. And I believe his murderer is still in that room. Well, let our name be vengeance then. Call Bradshaw." Bradshaw, the footman, came up. His face was white and nervous looking.

"Pull yourself together, Bradshaw," said Utterson. "Poole and I are going to force ourselves into the room. Meanwhile, if anyone should try to escape by the back, I want you there. You and the boy must get a pair of good sticks and wait by the back door. We will give you ten minutes to get to your stations."

Utterson and Poole sat down to wait beside the laboratory door. All around them, London hummed. But close at hand, the quiet was only broken by the footsteps moving to and fro along the laboratory floor.

"Is that the only sound you hear in there?" asked Utterson thoughtfully.

Poole said, "Once I heard weeping. Terrible weeping like that of a lost soul."

When the ten-minute wait drew to an end, Utterson called out in a loud voice. "Jekyll, I must and shall see you. If you refuse to let us in, we'll come in by force!"

A hoarse voice said, "Utterson! For God's sake, have mercy!"

"That's not Jekyll's voice —it's Hyde's!" Utterson cried. "Down with the door, Poole!"

Poole swung the axe. The blow shook the building. A screech, like that of an animal, rang out from the laboratory. Poole swung the axe again and again until the lock burst. At last the wreck of the door fell inward on the carpet.

Poole and Utterson looked into the laboratory. On the floor lay the body of a man, still twitching. They turned him over and looked on the face of Edward Hyde. He was dressed in clothes far too big for him. There was a small broken bottle in his hand. The smell of poison was in the air. It seemed that Hyde had killed himself.

"We have come too late to save or punish,"

Utterson said. "Now we must look for the body of your master."

Utterson and Poole looked in closets and the cellar. There was no trace of Dr. Jekyll, dead or alive. They looked all around the laboratory. On a long table, there were measured heaps of white crystals laid in glass saucers, as if for some experiment.

"That is the same drug I was always bringing him," said Poole.

On a shelf by the fire, Utterson found a holy book laid open. Someone had written dirty words on the pages—Hyde!

Also in the laboratory was a large mirror on one wall. Utterson and Poole looked into it with horror.

Poole whispered, "This glass has seen some strange things, sir."

"You may say that," agreed Poole.

Then, on a desk, they saw a large envelope with Mr. Utterson's name on it. Opening it up, Utterson saw Dr. Jekyll's will. But the terms in this will were different. Instead of Jekyll's property going to Mr. Hyde, he had given everything to Mr. Utterson!

Mr. Utterson looked at the body on the floor, then back at the will. He said, "Ah, Poole, my head goes round and round! Hyde has been here alone with the will for days. Why did he not destroy it?"

There was another paper in the envelope. It was a note from Dr. Jekyll. It read:

My Dear Utterson—When this note shall fall into your hands, I shall be gone. Go now, and read the letter Dr. Lanyon wrote you before he died. And if you care to hear more, you may read my confession.

Your unworthy and unhappy friend,
Henry Jekyll

"Was there something else in the envelope?" asked Mr. Utterson.

"Here, sir," said Poole. He handed Utterson a packet of papers.

Utterson said, "I must go home and read these in quiet. But I promise to be back before midnight. Then, Poole, we shall send for the police."

Locking the door behind him, Utterson set out for his office. Would the mysteries be explained when he read the two letters?

| 7 |

Dr. Lanyon's Story

Lanyon wrote that on the 9th of January he had received this letter from Dr. Jekyll:

Dear Lanyon—You are one of my oldest friends. Though we have often disagreed on scientific questions, I cannot remember any break in our friendship. If you depended on me, I would sacrifice my left hand to help you. Tonight, Lanyon—my life, my honor, and my very reason are all at your mercy. If you fail me tonight, I am lost.

I want you to put off all other plans for this evening. Take a cab to my house. Poole, my butler, will be waiting for you. He will take you to my laboratory. You are to go inside alone.

There you will find a desk with a glass front. I want you to take everything from the *fourth drawer from the top—**everything**. I beg of you to carry this back to your home.*

This is the first part of what I ask. Now for the second. If you get this letter in time, and set out for the laboratory at once, you should be back before midnight. I chose this late hour in case you run into difficulties. Also, I wish your servants to be in bed while you do the rest of what I ask.

At midnight, then, I ask you to be alone. A man, sent by me, will come to your door. Give him the contents of the drawer from my laboratory. Then you will have played your part—and earned my everlasting gratitude. Five minutes later, if you insist on an explanation, you will see why it was of such great importance.

Think of me, Lanyon, in a strange place, and in a blackness of distress. But if you will only help me, my troubles will roll away like a frightening story that ends well. Please serve me, my dear Lanyon, and save,

Your friend,

Henry Jekyll

Lanyon's letter to Utterson went on:

"On reading Jekyll's letter, I was sure that he must be insane. But until that could be proved, I felt bound to do as he asked. I got a cab and drove straight to his house where Poole was waiting for me. There I found a box in the drawer of his desk and brought it to my home.

"Once in my office, I opened the box and examined its contents. There were wrapped paper packets of white salt crystals and a small bottle containing a blood-red liquid, which had a strong smell. There was also a notebook. In it was written a series of dates that covered a period of many years. Here and there, Jekyll had written something next to one of the dates. Several times he had written the word *double*. Once, beside an early date, he had written, *total failure!!!*

"All this made my curiosity stronger, but told me little. The more I thought about it, the more certain I became that I was dealing with a diseased mind. I sent my servants to bed. Then I loaded an old revolver, in order to have some means of self defense.

"The clock had just struck midnight when I heard a gentle knock at the door.

" 'Who's there? Have you come from Dr. Jekyll?' I asked as I opened the door.

" 'Yes,' a man said, but he did not enter. Instead, he gave a look around and saw a policeman not far off. At the sight of the officer, the man hurried inside.

"The man's behavior made me uneasy. I kept my hand on my weapon as I followed him into my office. There, at last, I had a chance to see him clearly.

"There was something *awful* about the fellow that I could hardly name. He was a small man, dressed in clothes that were far too large for him. A normal man dressed this way would have been laughable. But there was nothing laughable about him. He was as abnormal as his clothes.

"The man was on fire with excitement. 'Have you got it? Have you got it?' he cried, grabbing my arm.

"At his touch, I felt an icy pang in my stomach. 'Come, sir,' I said. 'Be seated, if you please.'

" 'I beg your pardon, Dr. Lanyon. My impatience has made me forget my manners. I have come here on a piece of business for Dr. Jekyll. I understood . . . ' He stopped and put his hand on his throat. The man was trying to look calm, but I could see that he was almost hysterical. He went on, 'I understood, the contents of a drawer . . .'

" 'Yes, here it is, sir,' I said. I pointed to the box on my desk.

"He sprang forward to grab the box. But then he stopped and laid his hand on his heart. In the silence, I could hear his back teeth grinding against each other. The expression on his face was ghastly.

" 'Pull yourself together, sir!' I said.

"He turned to me with an awful smile and lifted the lid off the box. At the sight of the chemicals inside he gave a sob of relief. He asked, 'Have you a drinking glass?'

"I was almost too frightened to move, but I brought him what he wanted.

"He thanked me with a nod. Then he poured some of the red liquid into the glass. When he added one of the powders, the

mixture turned brighter. It began to fizz and throw off fumes. Then the mixture turned dark purple, and finally faded to a watery green. The man watched the chemical changes with a keen eye. Then he turned and looked at me closely.

" 'And now,' he said, 'do you wish to be wise? Will you leave me here with this glass in my hand? Or does curiosity have too strong a hold on you? If you leave me now, you will continue to be as you were before—no richer and no wiser. But if you stay, exciting new roads to knowledge, fame, and power shall be opened to you.'

"'Sir, you speak in riddles,' I said. 'I can hardly believe anything you say. But I have come too far to stop now. I must stay to see the end of this.'

"'Congratulations,' he said. 'Lanyon, your vision of medicine has always been far too narrow. You laughed at my ideas. Now you may see for yourself—and *believe*!'

"He put the glass to his lips and drank the potion in one gulp. Then he cried out, staggered for a moment, and grabbed at the end of the table. His body seemed to swell. His face suddenly became black. His very skin seemed to melt and change.

"The next moment, I sprang to my feet and jumped back against the wall. My mind sank in terror. I screamed again and again, *Oh, God! Oh, God!* For there before my eyes—pale and weak, like a man come back from the dead—was Henry Jekyll!

"What Henry Jekyll told me in the next hour, I cannot bear to write. *But I saw what I saw, and I heard what I heard.* It made my very soul sick. Even now that the sight has faded from my eyes, I cannot say that I truly believe it. My life is shaken to its roots. Sleep has left me. The most awful terror surrounds me day and night. I feel sure that my days on this earth are numbered.

"But I will say one thing, Utterson. The creature that came to my house that night was Hyde—the man hunted in every corner of the land for the murder of Carew."

Hastie Lanyon.

| 8 |

Henry Jekyll's Confession

"I was born in the 1800's. My family was rich. I was handsome and well-built. I was never afraid of hard work, and I wanted the respect of good people. It must seem that I had every guarantee of a fine future.

"My worst fault was that, secretly, I was sometimes wild. At the same time, however, I wanted to hold my head high and be respected by all. So I hid my love of pleasure and excitement. But as I grew older, I saw that I was living a double life.

"The low pleasures I tasted were nothing so terrible. But I was deeply ashamed of them, for I had set my standards so high.

"I thought much of this hard law of life: *While we long to reach high, we suffer for every stumble into sin.* How unhappy the struggle makes us!

"Though I led a double life, I was never a hypocrite. Both sides of me were very serious. I was perfectly true to myself when I put away control and plunged into sin. And I was just as much myself when I worked to help those in pain and suffering.

"My studies shed a strong light on the constant war between the good and evil in me. Every day brought me closer to the truth. It was this discovery that doomed me. For I have learned that a man is not really one, but *two*. I say two, because what I have learned does not pass beyond that point. Others who come after me will learn more. My guess is that one day man will be known to have *many* different sides.

"An idea took hold of me: If my two sides could be completely separate, I would suffer no longer. Evil could go its own way, free from the guilt of its high-minded twin. And good could walk its own upward path, no longer shamed by its evil side. It was the curse of mankind that these two were bound together. How, then, to separate them?

"My thoughts had already taken me far. But then I began to see an *answer* at my laboratory table. Certain chemicals have the power to shake up the flesh we wear, as easily as wind might toss a curtain.

"For two good reasons, I will not enter deeply into this part of my confession. First, I have learned that the heavy load we carry is forever fixed to our shoulders. If we try to throw it off, it returns—heavier than before. Second, as my story will make clear, my discoveries are not complete.

"Let me say only that I made a drug that separated the two sides of my spirit. The second man within me was just as real as the Henry Jekyll you know.

"I waited a long time before I put my ideas to the test. I knew well that I risked death. With any drug as powerful as this, a small overdose could kill me.

"But the temptation of such a great discovery finally overcame my fears. I had already begun to prepare the mixture. Now I bought a certain salt from the druggist. It was the last ingredient I needed.

"Then one cursed night, I mixed the ingredients together. I watched them bubble and smoke in the glass. When the bubbling died down, I drank the potion.

"The most racking pains followed immediately. My bones seemed to grind together. I felt deadly nausea and a horror of the spirit. Then, at last, I came to myself as if coming out of a great sickness.

"I felt something strange, something wonderfully new. I felt younger, lighter, and happier in body. A thrilling recklessness filled my mind. My soul felt free. I knew myself, at the first breath of this new life, to be more wicked—*ten times* more wicked. I stretched out my hands in pleasure. As I did this, I suddenly realized that I was smaller.

"At that time, there was no mirror in the laboratory. (Later, I brought one there to watch the powers of the potion.) I was determined to see myself in my bedroom mirror. The night was far gone into morning. Yet still the sky was black. The servants were in their deepest sleep.

"I crossed the yard. It seemed the stars

looked down in wonder at seeing the first creature of this kind. I crept from room to room, a stranger in my own house. Coming into my own bedroom and looking in the mirror, I saw for the first time—Edward Hyde.

"I do not know this for certain, but I think I can explain the reason for Hyde's small size. The evil side of my nature was smaller and less fully formed than the good. My life had been, after all, nine-tenths a life of effort, goodness, and control. And that, I think, is why Edward Hyde was lighter in build and younger than Henry Jekyll.

"The differences were clear to me. Just as goodness shone on the face of Henry Jekyll, evil was plainly written on the face of Edward Hyde. And yet when I looked on that ugly face in the mirror, I was not disgusted. Instead, my heart leaped up in welcome. This, too, was myself. It seemed natural and human. This evil being had a livelier spirit than the divided and imperfect self I had always known.

"I soon noticed other differences. When I went about as Edward Hyde, I made people extremely uncomfortable. This reaction, I believe, is due to the fact that all humans are a mixture of good and evil. Edward Hyde, on the other hand, was alone in the ranks of mankind. He was pure evil.

"I stayed but a moment in front of the mirror. The second part of the experiment had yet to be tried. It might be possible that I had lost my old self forever! If so, I would have to run away before daylight. How could I stay in a house that was no longer mine?

"I hurried back to the laboratory. Once more, I prepared and drank the potion. Once more I suffered the pains. But in a moment I came to myself again with the body and face of Henry Jekyll.

"That night I had come to a fatal crossroads. If I had made my experiment in a noble spirit, the potion might have made me an angel instead of a monster. The *potion* did not decide whom I would become. It only shook open the doors of my personality and let loose what was inside. As Edward Hyde, all that was good in me slept. My evil side was awake and ready to seize its chance.

"My new power tempted me until I fell

into slavery. All I had to do was drink from the glass. Then I could toss away the body of the respected doctor and become Edward Hyde. Just the idea of it made me smile.

"I prepared myself with great care. I took that house in Soho, where Hyde was tracked by the police. As Jekyll, I told my servants that Hyde was to come and go as he pleased. I made out that will, which bothered you so much, Utterson. If anything happened to Jekyll, I wanted to be sure Hyde lost no money or property.

"Many men have hired others to commit their crimes, while keeping their own reputation safe. For me, the safety was *complete*. Think of it—I did not even exist! I could escape through my laboratory door, swallow the potion, and Edward Hyde would pass away, like breath upon a mirror.

"The wild excitement I looked for as Edward Hyde was already low enough. But soon I became monstrous. When I came back from those bad nights I was filled with wonder at my wickedness. Every act I did as Hyde was centered on myself. I took pleasure from any kind of torture to others. I was a man with a heart made of stone.

"Henry Jekyll was horrified at the behavior of Edward Hyde. But it was Hyde, after all, and Hyde alone, who was guilty. Jekyll was not hurt. He woke in the morning with his good qualities untouched. If possible, he would even undo the evil done by Hyde. And so his conscience slept.

"I have no wish to write the details of the evil I have done. I only wish to show how I was warned that I would be punished in the end.

"Not long ago I had an accident. Edward Hyde ran over a child in the street. Your cousin, Enfield, saw the act and caught me. The child's family and the doctor joined him. Their anger against me was so great that I feared for my life.

"To satisfy them, Edward Hyde had to bring them to the laboratory door. Then he paid them off with a check drawn in the name of Henry Jekyll. I made sure I would never open myself to such danger of discovery in the future. I opened an account at another bank in the name of Edward Hyde. By sloping my writing backward, I gave my other self a signature. I thought I was then beyond the reach of fate.

"Some two months before the murder of Sir Danvers Carew, I stayed out late on one of my adventures as Hyde. The next day, I woke feeling odd. Something kept telling me I was not in my own home, but in the little room in Soho. I would sleep in Soho when I was in the body of Edward Hyde. I smiled to myself, and dropped back into a comfortable doze.

"When I woke up my eyes fell upon my hand. As you know, the hand of Henry Jekyll was large, firm, white, and handsome. But the hand I now saw was lean and covered with a thick growth of hair. It was the hand of Edward Hyde!

"I must have stared at it, stupidly, for nearly half a minute. Then terror exploded in my chest like the crash of cymbals. I leapt up from the bed and rushed to the mirror. What I saw made my heart stop beating! Yes, I had gone to bed as Henry Jekyll—and woken up as Edward Hyde.

| 9 |

A Fateful Crossroads

"What should I do? Now it was well on into the morning. The servants were up. All my drugs were shut away in my laboratory.

"Then I remembered, with sweet relief, that the servants were already used to my second self. I quickly dressed, as well as I was able, in Henry Jekyll's clothes.

"Bradshaw drew back in surprise at seeing me pass through the house. Why was Edward Hyde up at this early hour, and so strangely dressed? I went on into the laboratory. Ten minutes later, Dr. Jekyll had returned to his own shape and was pretending to eat his breakfast.

"My appetite was small indeed. This sudden change into Hyde seemed to spell out the letters of my judgment. I thought more seriously than ever before about the dangers of my leading a double life.

"It seemed that the spirit of Edward Hyde was growing stronger. What would I do if Hyde grew more and more powerful? What if I became him forever?

"The drug had not always worked as perfectly as I had wished. In one of my early experiments, it had failed me totally. More than once I had been forced to double the dose to make it work. In the beginning, the difficulty had been to change into Edward Hyde. Now the difficulty was to throw off the body of Hyde. *I was slowly losing hold of my better self.*

"Between these two, I had to choose. Jekyll looked on and shared the adventures of Hyde. But Hyde cared nothing for Jekyll. Hyde looked on Jekyll as a bandit looks on a cave in which to hide. Jekyll had more than a father's interest in Hyde. But Hyde had more than a selfish son's indifference.

"To cast my lot with Jekyll was to lose the secret pleasures I enjoyed. To stay with Hyde was to become hated and friendless. Finally I chose the better part of me. But I did not have the strength to hold on.

"Yes, I preferred the elderly, restless Dr. Jekyll. I preferred to be surrounded by friends, holding fast to my honest hopes. I said goodbye to the wild, young Hyde.

"Yet perhaps a small part of me held onto Hyde. For I still kept the house in Soho. I also kept Edward Hyde's clothes.

"For two months, I lived a life that was good and pure. I had never been more severe with myself. I was free from guilt, and it was a feeling I enjoyed.

"But before long the fear of losing Henry Jekyll began to fade away. The evil Hyde was longing for freedom! So once again, in an hour of weakness, I mixed and swallowed the potion.

"My devil had been caged for a long time. Now he came out roaring. Even as I swallowed the drug, I knew that I was far more evil than ever before.

"It was in this mood of savagery that I met Sir Danvers Carew on the street that night. That innocent man did nothing but ask for directions. Yet I struck him down—just as a child in a tantrum might break a toy! The spirit of hell raged inside me. I struck Carew's body again and again. I tasted delight in every blow.

"Only when I became tired did I stop. Then, with a cold thrill of terror, I realized that my life was in danger. I ran from the scene. My love of life was screwed to the topmost peg.

"When I reached my house in Soho, I burned my papers. Then I set out again through the lighted streets. I gloried in my crime, and thought of more evil I might do in the future.

"I reached the laboratory and prepared the potion. Hyde drank the drug with a song on his lips. The pain of the drug's changes was still with him when Henry Jekyll sank to his knees. With tears of thanks for his escape, he lifted his hands to God.

"For the first time I saw my life as a whole. I followed it from the days of childhood, when I had walked holding my father's hand. I thought of my years of hard work as a doctor. I could have screamed out loud. With tears and prayers, I tried to smother out the awful sights and sounds of the murder.

"Then, as the pain of guilt began to die away, it was replaced by a sense of joy. I could never be Hyde again. I was locked forever in the better part of myself.

"The next day, the news of the murder was out. I learned that the victim had been Sir Danvers Carew, M.P. The police searched for Hyde in every corner of the land. This I was glad to know. Now my better self was guarded by fear of death. Jekyll was now my city of safety. If Hyde peeped out for only an instant, the hands of all men would raise up to kill him.

"I vowed that my work in the future would redeem my past. I can honestly say I did a fair amount of good. You know, Utterson, how hard I worked last year to help those who were suffering. You know how much I did for others. My days passed quietly. I was almost happy.

"Yet I still had my evil side. Once the first edge of guilt wore off, that dark side longed for freedom. Of course, I never dreamed of bringing back Hyde. The very idea chilled my blood. No, it was as Henry Jekyll that I looked for pleasure. Now I was an ordinary secret sinner, like so many men among us.

"But my romance with evil had begun the end of me. It finally destroyed the balance of my soul.

"It happened on a fine, clear day in January. I was in Regent's Park, sitting in the sun. The animal within me was licking its chops, remembering the low pleasures I had recently tasted. My better side was drowsy, not yet awake.

"I was thinking how much I was like my neighbors. Yet no, I thought, I was even *better*—because I worked so hard at doing good. Suddenly, a horrid nausea came over me. Then I felt a deathly shuddering. These feelings passed away and left me faint.

"A change had taken place in my thoughts. Now I felt bold. Danger seemed nothing to me. I looked down. My clothes hung loosely on my body. The hand that lay on my knee was hairy.

I was once more Edward Hyde.

"A moment before I had been safe in the respect of all men. I had been wealthy and beloved. Now I was homeless—and a hunted murderer!

"My drugs were in my laboratory cabinet. How was I to reach them? If I entered the house, my servants would send me to the gallows. I saw I must make use of another man's hand. I thought of Lanyon.

"I called a passing cab. Of course my clothes were far too large. The driver could not keep from laughing at me. I bared my teeth at him like a mad dog. The smile quickly shrank from his face.

"I drove to an inn. Entering, I gave everyone there such black looks that they quickly turned away. I was led to a private room, and given paper and a pen.

"Hyde in danger was a creature new to me. He was gripped by anger. He longed to give pain. Yet he was sharp in mind. He controlled his anger with great effort of will.

"He wrote two important letters: one to Lanyon and one to Poole. Then he sat all day by the fire in a private room. He paced up and down and chewed his nails. At dinner he sat alone with his fears. The waiter trembled as he set down his food.

"When night finally came, he took a closed cab and drove about the city. *He*, I say—I cannot say *I*. That child of hell was nothing human. Nothing lived in him but fear and hatred.

"Finally, he paid the cab and set out on foot. He walked fast, hunted by his fears. He counted the minutes that still divided him from midnight. Once a woman spoke to him. I think she wanted to sell him a box of matches. He hit her in the face, and she ran away.

"At last it was midnight. I came to myself at Lanyon's. My old friend was filled with horror for me. I knew he was condemning me, but I heard his words as if in a dream. And it was partly in a dream that I returned to my own house and got into bed. Even my nightmares could not wake me.

"I hated and feared the brute that slept inside me. I had not forgotten the dangers of the day before. But I was once more in my own home. I was close to my drugs. I was so thankful for my escape that I felt almost hopeful.

"After breakfast I was walking outside when once again I felt the change coming on. I had just enough time to run to my laboratory before I had turned into Hyde. This time it took a double dose to bring me back to myself. Alas! Six hours later, I was looking into the fire when the pains returned. Once again I had to take the drug.

From that day on, it was only by great effort that I was able to wear the face of Henry Jekyll at all. At every hour of the day and night, Hyde threatened to return. If I slept, or even dozed for a moment, I would wake up as Edward Hyde.

"I could not sleep. I was eaten up by fever and weak both in body and mind. There was a single thought in my head—a horror of forever becoming my other self!

"Now the change from Jekyll to Hyde hardly gave me any pain at all. When I slept, or the drug wore off, I slipped easily into the body of Hyde. As Jekyll became sicker and weaker, Hyde grew ever stronger.

"Just as Jekyll hates and fears Hyde, Hyde hates Jekyll also. He plays rude, ape-like tricks, such as writing dirty words in Jekyll's holy book.

"Hyde would have destroyed me long ago, except that he, too, would have to die with me. I know how much he fears my power to cut him off by suicide. Sometimes I even find it in my heart to pity him.

"The struggle between Hyde and myself might have gone on for years. But now, it comes to an end. The salt that I needed to make the drug is nearly gone. When I first noticed the supply was running low, I ordered more. I mixed the potion and drank it—but nothing happened. I sent Poole out again and again to find a new supply of the salt, but my efforts were useless. I am now certain that the first supply I used was impure. Whatever was in the old salt had made the drug work.

"In order to finish this writing, I have now taken the last of the drug. I must hurry, for if Hyde takes over while I am writing, he will surely tear this letter to pieces.

"Half an hour from now, I shall be Hyde forever. Will Hyde be hung for the murder of Carew? Or will he find the courage to kill himself before he is captured? I cannot say. Only God knows.

"This is my true hour of death. What follows does not concern me, but only Edward Hyde. Here then, I lay down my pen and seal up this confession. The unhappy life of Henry Jekyll is at an end."

Activities
Dr. Jekyll and Mr. Hyde

BOOK SEQUENCE

First complete the sentences with words from the box. Then number the events to show which happened first, second, and so on.

confession	peace	terms	trampling	visit
laboratory	address	crime	examines	obey
handwriting	hiding	truth	nightmares	

____ 1. Mr. Guest studies two _____ samples.

____ 2. Poole asks Utterson to _____ Jekyll's house.

____ 3. Hyde writes down his _____ for Mr. Utterson.

____ 4. Enfield sees a man _____ on a child's body.

____ 5. Mr. Utterson reads Henry Jekyll's _____.

____ 6. Poole says the servants have orders to _____ Mr. Hyde.

____ 7. Utterson has strange _____ about his friend Jekyll.

____ 8. For two months, Dr. Jekyll seems to be at _____.

____ 9. From her window, a young maid sees a _____ committed.

____ 10. Utterson sees that Jekyll has changed the _____ of his will.

____ 11. Poole uses an axe to break down the _____ door.

____ 12. Inspector Newcomen _____ Hyde's rooms in Soho.

____ 13. Utterson asks Jekyll if he is _____ Mr. Hyde.

____ 14. Lanyon says that Utterson will learn the _____ only after he is dead.

IDIOMS

Reread Chapter 1 and circle a letter to show the meaning of each **boldfaced** phrase.

1. Mr. Utterson's friends were those of **his own blood,** or those he had known the longest.
   a. with whom he had made a blood oath
   b. of his own blood type
   c. family members related by blood

2. Mr. Richard Enfield was a well-known **man about town**.
   a. a worldly fellow seen in fashionable places
   b. a man who owned many houses in town
   c. one who knew many facts about the town

3. Utterson's and Enfield's friendship was a **nut to crack** for many.
   a. as tough as nutshell
   b. hard to understand
   c. worth opening

4. The family's doctor was about **as emotional as a bagpipe**.
   a. stiff, not showing passion
   b. whining and piping
   c. wild and free

5. Enfield promised Hyde that he would **make his name stink** from one end of London to the other.
   a. People would hold their noses when they said his name.
   b. tell everyone what he had done
   c. make fun of his name

6. Enfield **took to his heels** and seized the man by the collar.
   a. leaned back on his heels
   b. grabbed his shoes
   c. started to run

82

7. Although Hyde was frightened, he was **carrying it off like Satan**.

    a. carrying stolen money in his pockets

    b. acting as boldly as the devil

    c. trying to run off down the street

INFERENCE

Reread Chapter 3 and circle a letter to show the *implied* (not literally stated) meaning of each sentence from the story.

1. **After Jekyll's lighthearted and loose-tongued guests had gone, he liked the silent companionship of the old lawyer.**

    a. Jekyll secretly despised his oldest acquaintances.

    b. Jekyll regretted inviting so many guests.

    c. Utterson required little attention or conversation.

2. **Regarding the terms of his will, Jekyll says that it is "one of those affairs that cannot be mended by talking."**

    a. He knew that Utterson would be able to offer no useful advice.

    b. He thought that talking to a lawyer was much too expensive.

    c. His friendship with Hyde was broken and could not be mended.

3. **Jekyll tells Utterson, "I cannot find words to thank you."**

    a. He's having trouble remembering hard words.

    b. In fact he is not grateful at all.

    c. The depth of his gratitude is difficult to express.

4. **On the subject of his will, Jekyll begs Utterson to "let the matter slip."**
   a. Utterson should stay up all night and think about it.
   b. Utterson should never say another word about it.
   c. In his sleep, Jekyll hopes to come up with an answer.

5. **Jekyll says it would be "a weight off his mind" if Utterson would promise to help Hyde.**
   a. It would relieve him of a burdensome worry.
   b. It would help him to lose weight in his face.
   c. His brain had grown too large and heavy.

COMPREHENSION CHECK
Reread Chapters 4 and 5 and answer below.

A. Circle a letter to show how each sentence should be completed.

1. **In his letter, Jekyll urged Utterson to**
   a. never doubt their friendship.
   b. blame Lanyon for the problem.

2. **After Dr. Lanyon's funeral, Utterson**
   a. locked up Lanyon's letter without reading it.
   b. quickly read Lanyon's long letter about Henry Jekyll.

3. **Poole told Utterson that Dr. Jekyll**
   a. often went out walking with Mr. Enfield.
   b. spent most of his time in his laboratory.

4. **Enfield felt sure that he and Utterson**
   a. had seen the last of Mr. Hyde.
   b. should break into Jekyll's laboratory.

84

5. **When Utterson told Jekyll he "should get his blood moving," he meant that Jekyll**
   a. needed more blood pressure medicine.
   b. ought to get out for some exercise.

B. Dr. Jekyll felt sick and shaken when he heard the news of Carew's murder. **Have you ever been shocked and sickened by a news item? What was the news? Why did it have such a great effect on you?**

I was shocked when I heard that _____

_____

_____

Because _____

_____

_____

FIGURATIVE LANGUAGE

Reread Chapter 8. Then circle a letter to show the literal meaning of each **boldface** phrase below.

1. As I grew older, I saw that I was **living a double life**.
   a. lived in two different countries
   b. behaved both very well and very badly

2. My studies **shed a strong light** on the constant war between the good and evil in me.
   a. revealed the reason behind
   b. created an electrical glow

3. I learned that the heavy load we human beings must carry is **forever fixed to our shoulders**.
   a. never removed from us
   b. loaded in a backpack

4. I waited a long time before I **put my ideas to the test**.

   a. tested other's knowledge of them

   b. tried them out

5. Edward Hyde was **alone in the ranks of mankind**.

   a. the only purely evil human

   b. the usual mix of bad and good

6. That night I **had come to a fatal crossroads**.

   a. realized that I would die any day now

   b. was faced with a life-or-death decision

7. Finding pleasure in torturing others, I was a **man of stone**.

   a. uncaring, unfeeling

   b. rocklike, without flesh

8. Because Dr. Jekyll's good qualities were untouched, **his conscience slept**.

   a. He was tormented by shame.

   b. He felt no guilt.

FINAL EXAM

Circle a letter to correctly answer each question or complete each statement.

1. What did Utterson mean by saying, "I let my brother go to the devil in his own way."?

   a. He didn't intrude on other people's business.

   b. He wasn't willing to help people in trouble.

   c. He believed that his brother worshipped the devil.

   d. He feared that his friends were headed for hell.

2. What did Dr. Lanyon think about Edward Hyde?
   a. He found him detestable in every way.
   b. He thought Hyde was bold and exciting.
   c. He declared that he had never heard of him.
   d. He was frightened to death of him.

3. How did the police know that Sir Danvers Carew had not been killed in a robbery?
   a. No robbery had been reported.
   b. Carew was too shabbily dressed to attract a robber.
   c. Carew was mistaken for someone else.
   d. A purse and a fine gold watch were in Carew's pockets.

4. Poole said that if Jekyll invited Utterson into his lab, Utterson should
   a. rush in and save him.
   b. stay outside.
   c. refuse to answer.
   d. break down the door.

5. When Poole and Utterson broke into the laboratory, they saw
   a. a broken bottle clutched in Hyde's hand.
   b. Bradshaw hiding in a corner.
   c. that Jekyll's equipment had been destroyed.
   d. Hyde leaping out at them.

6. Jekyll's letter instructed Lanyon to
   a. put an end to Edward Hyde.
   b. bring the police to his laboratory.
   c. sell his valuable belongings.
   d. take things from a desk drawer.

Answers to Activities
Dr. Jekyll and Mr. Hyde

BOOK SEQUENCE
1. 8/handwriting   2. 11/visit   3. 3/address
4. 1/trampling   5. 14/confession   6. 4/obey
7. 2/nightmares   8. 9/peace   9. 5/crime
10. 13/terms   11. 12/laboratory   12. 6/examines
13. 7/hiding   14. 10/truth

IDIOMS
1. c   2. a   3. b   4. a   5. b   6. c   7. b

INFERENCE
1. c   2. a   3. c   4. b   5. a

COMPREHENSION CHECK
A. 1. a   2. a   3. b   4. a   5. b
B. Answers will vary.

FIGURATIVE LANGUAGE
1. b   2. a   3. a   4. b   5. a   6. b   7. a   8. b

FINAL EXAM: 1. a   2. c   3. d   4. b   5. a   6. d